Murder in the Val D'Elsa

by David Sellar

DORRANCE
PUBLISHING CO
EST. 1920
PITTSBURGH, PENNSYLVANIA 15238

Dorrance Publishing Co
585 Alpha Drive
Pittsburgh, PA 15238
Visit our website at *www.dorrancebookstore.com*

ISBN: 979-8-8852-7010-6
eISBN: 979-8-8852-7740-2

Dedicated to Stefano Marrano, Joost Moolhuijzen and
Carolyn Maxwell-Mahon for their wonderful editing and love

Chapter One
Sunday and Monday

Mark and his good friend Andrew were sitting on a flight from Barcelona to Florence. Both of them had flown into Barcelona, Mark from San Francisco where he worked at Williams-Sonoma, and Andrew from Minneapolis where he worked at Eli Lilly.

They had planned a trip to Barcelona to get on a cruise ship to go around the Mediterranean but with two months' notice the cruise was cancelled and their good friend Jim had left the ship. So since the guys had already booked plane flights, they decided to still meet up in Barcelona, and then Mark found an Airbnb place in a little town called Barberino Val D'Elsa in Tuscany. It looked adorable and they booked it instantly.

The PA came on as they were approaching Florence airport:

> *Signore e signori, purtroppo il nostro volo è stato dirottato su Bologna come ci sono fulmini e tuoni a causa di una perturbazione con tuoni e fulmini su firenze. Arriveremo a Bologna in fra quindici minuti. La compagnia aerea organizzerà il trasporto a Firenze. Grazie per aver volato con Vueling Airways.*

And then in promising English:

Lady and gentleman, unfortunately our flight diverted will be as there is thunder lightning over Firenze. We will arrive at Bologna in fifteen minutes. Airline will arrange transport to Firenze airport. Thank you for flying Vueling Airways.

Since the boys were apparently the only passengers on the small plane that spoke English, and their grasp of Italian was limited, they decided to wait until they got to Bologna and see what eventuated. They did not know quite what to expect but travel throws you curve-balls. They were due at the Airbnb property at 3:00 P.M. and since it was 1:30 P.M. now they thought they wouldn't be overly late to meet with the owner at his home in Tavarnelle which was a couple of miles north of Barberino.

Mark and Andrew had not expected the delays that were inevitable. It took ninety minutes for the airport to arrange a coach to take all the passengers from Bologna airport to Florence airport. On the way, they encountered an episode of the traditional Italian road rage including a stop mid-freeway with two coach drivers arguing violently with each other. Finally the coach took off again and pulled into a roadside roadstop and layby where the *polizia* were waiting. They joined the other passengers outside the coach and milled around for thirty minutes while the *polizia* argued, again violently, with the driver. After that time with apparently good wishes all around, the driver signaled that all passengers should get back on the coach. The next stage of the journey was ravishing for Mark as he had never been to Italy before – a scene of parks, mountains, serene valleys, ruined castles and farmhouses with the occasional cow.

Arriving at Florence Amerigo Vespucci airport, the coach discharged its passengers and the boys wandered over to the Hertz rental counter, a little shack in the middle of a car park. They had booked a Mercedes sedan for the week with automatic transmission (something that Andrew insisted upon, rather than a manual). After some language and financial issues, including a testy call to Andrew's bank in the U.S., all was resolved, the deal was complete and with keys in hand they found the car. Mark had brought along a printed out Google map of how to get from Florence to Barberino but the road system was so different from America that they took the E25 motorway instead of the SR2 highway, hilariously nicknamed the Siena-Firenze highway or Si-Fi.

After a couple of hours Mark suggested to Andrew that they might be lost so they pulled off the motorway and found themselves at the parking lot of a dodgy-looking bar and restaurant. It was 8:00 P.M. by this stage so they decided to have a break from driving and get some food. The restaurant presented a roadhouse look – Mark thought that it was a scene where there might be biker gangs hanging around. When the guys entered, the *patroni* looked at them in an unfriendly manner but the bartender was surprisingly nice and helpful. It turned out that the kitchen had closed but the bartender offered to make the guys some sandwiches, which were surprisingly good. While he was chatting in reasonable English at the table, Mark asked him how to get to Barberino with the now-useless Google map.

The bartender was amused and said, 'Are you sure you want to do this? It's nighttime and it's mountainous but there is a road to get there….' He drew the road on the map, then brought out a better map of his own, consulted some of the *patroni* who assured everyone that it was achievable, and the boys agreed to try it. Mark called the Airbnb host to assure him that they were on the road and the owner, Paolo, said just to call in at his house any time – it didn't matter how late it was.

The guys took off again after a bathroom break and entered unwillingly and a little afraid into the challenge. They soon found the road and started up the mountains. It was very dark but exciting and scenic. They passed Badia a Coltibuono, the ancestral home of Lorenza de Medici whose cooking show on PBS Mark had watched avidly in the past. It was beautifully flood lit and looked romantic and very medieval. They passed Radda in Chianti, Panzano and Fabbrica until they came to the Si-Fi highway. They found the turn off for Tavarnelle and decided to drive to Barberino and find the house. That part was easy….although there was nobody there to welcome them. Mark said that they should drive back to Tavarnelle and find Paolo's house and see if they could get the key. It was about 11:00 P.M. at this stage and confident that Paolo had said, 'Come any time,' they did that. Finding the right address, Mark knocked on the front door – loudly and frequently, with no response. This went on for quite some time with more trips between Tavarnelle and Barberino so as 1:30 A.M. approached, the guys had seen a resort hotel on the road called the Borgo di Cortefreda. Eventually with no success in knocking up Paolo, the guys decided to call into the Borgo and see if there were rooms available. Mark went into the lobby while Andrew stayed in the car in case nothing was available, but successfully obtained two rooms in this lovely historic-looking but modern hotel. The desk clerk was surprised at the late arrival but offered the rooms for € 100 each and Mark threw his Amex card at him with gratitude and tiredness.

The guys settled down in their rooms, and next morning (well, the same morning now) Mark walked out on his private patio and sat in the warm August sunshine. They had breakfast about 8:00 A.M. which was delicious. 'Mark, can we just stay here instead?' said Andrew. Although that was tempting Mark called Paolo later that morning, after a wonderful swim in the hotel's pool, overlooking valleys and hills with castles, olive groves and vineyards, and agreed to meet at the Airbnb in Barberino at 11:00 A.M.

After introducing themselves to Paolo, he asked, 'Why didn't you stop by last night?' Their responses were interesting and frustrated.

However, they soon settled in to the place, a tiny home over three levels which had been built into the inside of the old town wall. The ground floor was the kitchen and living room. The second floor had the first bedroom and bathroom and the third floor had the second bedroom and bathroom. Above that was a roof deck which overlooked the street. Barberino is about 1000 years old and was a half-way point between Florence and Siena. The guys decided to take a walk through the one skinny main street – just wide enough to fit a FIAT *bambino* as it was really designed for a horse or donkey and cart. They ended at a small *enoteca* where there were three items on the menu – tomato bruschetta, a salad and a soup. They enjoyed the bruschetta which was a revelation for American tastes as it was simple and mind-blowingly delicious.

After lunch the boys wandered through the town and found the church, the Chiesa Parrocchiale di San Bartolomeo, two of the three restaurants that the town boasted, and a bar called Crazy Bar. They returned to what was now home and passed a relaxing afternoon. Mark went to park the Mercedes in a side street down the hill a little as it was impossible to drive it through the main part of town or park outside the house.

That night the guys went to the pizza restaurant in the town square called Pico and enjoyed every bite. The food in Italy was proving to be a life-changing experience.

Chapter Two

Tuesday

The next morning the guys planned to go to the supermarket in Tavarnelle to stock up on coffee and snacks to supplement the very tasty food that they had already tried. Mark walked down to where the car was parked and saw a man lying on top of the bonnet. He looked like he was trying to steal the three-pointed star emblem off the front, but as Mark got closer he saw that the man was motionless. Walking right up to the car, Mark then saw that there was a most effective bullet hole in the back of the man's head, with a little blood surrounding it.

Mark knew enough from detective stories to not touch the body, but he did check for the man's pulse although wasn't sure that he'd done it correctly. In any case, a bullet hole like that wouldn't admit any life. The man looked vaguely familiar but Mark couldn't place him just then.

He ran up to the house and called 112 on his cell phone, not sure if it would work in Italy.

'*Si, buon giorno – qual è la tua emergenza urgenza?*'

'Buon giorno – Inglese?' asked Mark, not hoping to make the question sound reasonable.

'Yes, signor, how can I help you?'

'There's been an accident and a man is dead. Well, actually it looks like a murder.'

'Where are you, signor?'

'Barberino in the Chianti region…we're staying in a house near the Siena Gate of the town.'

'What is the address please?'

'I don't really know…..it's a three-story house built into the town wall just at the southern end of the main street.'

'Very well signor, please stay there and we'll find you. What is your name?'

'Mark Wendell.'

Mark called out to Andrew who was still upstairs in his bedroom. 'Andrew, come down!'

When Andrew arrived in the kitchen, Mark said, 'There's been a murder and the body is lying on the car. And – holy shit – it's Paolo!' suddenly realizing what he had seen.

Andrew said, reasonably enough, 'Are you drunk?'

'Not yet but I feel like I am.'

'Here – have some wine and you'll feel better.' They found some leftover wine in the refrigerator, presumably from the previous guests, and Mark drank some. Andrew did not drink alcohol.

Medicine administered, the boys sat on the front step and fifteen minutes later an Alfa Romeo with blue lights flashing pulled around the triangular corner on which the house was situated. Mark waved his arms and a man in plain clothes and a uniformed policeman parked in the middle of the narrow road with the blue lights still flashing and approached them.

'*Buon giorno*, signor, are you signor Wendess?' said the plain-clothes man.

'Yes I am but it's Wendell.'

'Please spell that for me.' Mark did.

'Where is this alleged dead body, signor?'

'Follow me and I will take you there. It's only a two-minute walk.'

Suiting action to word the two *polizi* and Mark walked down to where the car was parked. On the way Mark admired the cut of the plainclothes man's suit, his wide shoulders and slim hips. The man's face was craggy and somewhat lined but handsome enough, with the blue eyes that are often found in northern Italians. He had dark blond hair, appeared to be in his early thirties and was very tall, towering over Mark's six feet height.

'What is your name, *Ispettore*?' Mark said, hoping that was the correct rank and address.

'I am Ispettore Garibaldi and this is my associate, Carabiniere Sugo.' Mark thought that the correct address would have been *tenante* but didn't have enough confidence to ask.

Mark had an internal battle not to laugh at the name Garibaldi, thinking of high school history lessons, and Sugo, casting his mind back to Italian cookbooks he owned, but managed to control it.

'Well, gentlemen, you can see for yourself what I found,' as they walked up to the car with the body atop it.

As they spoke, another siren and set of lights rolled up with Carabiniere Sugo giving instructions on his *cellulare* to what turned out to be an ambulance.

'You're shaking, signor,' said Garibaldi to Mark, 'go back to the house and please wait there for us.'

Mark had not realized that he had been shaking but took the advice. By this time Andrew had just crossed the road and was approaching the car park so Mark collected him and they returned to the house.

'Mark, are you sure that's Paolo?' said Andrew.

'I think so but he was face down so I'm not 100 percent sure.'

'Wow, that's creepy. Sounds so inadequate but it's just…..' Andrew failed to find the right words.

'I know, I know,' said Mark.

After about an hour, the Ispettore and Carabiniere Sugo came back to the house and knocked before asking permission to enter the open front door. The ambulance's siren was heard again driving away although that seemed unnecessary now. Mark and Andrew asked the policemen to sit down at the small table in the kitchen and offered some refreshment but that was declined.

'I have some questions for you, signor,' said the Ispettore addressing Mark.

'Certainly. Ask away.'

'The deceased is a gentleman named Paolo Nunienzo. He died of a bullet to the back of the head, as you probably saw. The medical examiner has taken the body back to the morgue. Did you happen to know this gentleman?'

'Yes, well, sort of. He's the owner of this property which we are in, and we met him yesterday to get the keys. He lives – I mean lived – in Tavarnelle but when we tried to contact him on Sunday night he was…umm…unavailable.'

'Unavailable, signor?' said the Ispettore.

'Yes – well it was kind of a cluster all round but…'

'A 'cluster', signor?'

'Meaning it was a mess and we couldn't get in here on the night that we intended. Sorry, it's a rude Americanism.'

'Ah, *grazie*…so where did you stay on that evening when you had the – err – issues?'

'At the Borgo di Cortefreda just down the road.'

'I don't know that – I'm from Firenze so I don't know this area all that well. Do you know this hotel, Sugo?'

'*Si, signor. Posso portartici.*'

'Okay – *grazie* Signor Wendell and Signor Smith. We will pursue our enquiries and may have more questions for you. In the meantime may I take a look at your passports *per favor*?'

Mark and Andrew produced the passports which were duly noted and scanned with a portable device attached to an iPad that Sugo held. The policemen returned the passports, thanked the guys again and departed.

'Ispettore – are we free to – ummm – move around and resume our vacation?' asked Mark.

'Vacation, signor?'

'Holiday I meant to say.'

'Oh, si, si signor. But please don't leave the country.'

'Okay – thank you gentlemen.' The policemen departed and Andrew saw that some of the village locals had gathered around the Alfa thinking that there was something scandalous to see. The crowd melted away after the blue lights and handsome policemen had left.

Chapter Three
Tuesday

Andrew and Mark took the Mercedes out once the police and medical attendants had left. They were a little wary of any blood splashes on the rental car but it seemed perfectly normal. They drove into Tavarnelle to the Coop supermarket and bought wine, coffee, beer and chocolates. Mark was fascinated by the difference between Italian and American supermarkets…it was all cash – no cards, no checks, no coupons – and he found that Italian housewives buy Barilla pasta which came as somewhat of a pleasant surprise. They found an ATM and pulled out some Euro, even with the difficulty of reading the instructions in Italian, and finally filled up the car with petrol.

That night the boys walked down the street about half a mile to a restaurant that they had seen two nights before on their seemingly endless commute between Barberino and Tavarnelle. It was called Il Paese dei Campanelli, presumably because it was within the sound of the bells of the Chiesa Parrocchiale di San Bartolomeo in the village.

Mark and Andrew were greeted by a statuesque, slim, vision of Italian style of a certain age wearing an immaculate Armani suit, her hair beautifully dressed and her jewelry magnificent but downplayed. Mark immediately named her 'The Contessa' in his mind. Her name was Giulia, she told the boys, and with flawless English she found a table for the two.

They ordered magnificent meals from the menu, including a white pizza which Andrew favored as he found red tomato sauce to be too acid. Mark had gnocchi with a tasty Bolognese sauce. The Contessa hovered discreetly without interrupting, maintaining an orderly well-run restaurant and walking around supervising her team on six-inch heels, the service was attentive and the food exceeded expectation. The wine that Mark ordered was local and delicious. It was a relaxed and slow meal which the boys appreciated after the excitement and horror of the morning, which seemed remote the more time wore on.

The boys went for a walk through the village when they got home and decided to try Crazy Bar, but it was locked up and dark. They continued walking and went through the Florence Gate on the north side of the village to another bar called The Bar. It was tiny and cute. Mark bought a liter of white wine for himself and a glass of mineral water for Andrew and went to sit outside. There was a group of old gentlemen playing cards and dominos on a couple of tables, and in the gathering gloom of the evening the boys could see all the wives sitting opposite The Bar in the local cemetery – sitting on the grave-stones – gossiping but keeping an eye on their men to ensure they didn't misbehave. Young couples on Vespas roared past enjoying the freedom of riding skin to skin with their crushes and not wearing crash helmets in the warm summer night. A couple of mosquitos landed and were quickly extinguished and the stars were very clear as the night darkened.

The boys walked home when the wine was finished and passing through the Florence Gate and then the Siena Gate were enchanted by the mellow limestone buildings in the moonlight and the odd street light along the tiny main thoroughfare casting pools of illumination. They slept exceedingly well.

Chapter Four
Wednesday

The next morning, Wednesday, dawned sunny and warm. Mark and Andrew enjoyed coffee and mineral water on the roof deck looking out over the few streets of the village and the light morning traffic.

At 9:00 A.M. the doorbell rang so Mark went downstairs to find out who it was – it was Ispettore Garibaldi, wearing another impeccably tailored suit.

'*Buon giorno*, signore, may I come in? I have some more questions for you.'

'Of course, Ispettore…would you like a coffee?'

'An espresso please.'

Suiting action at the Keurig to the request, Mark sat down with the Ispettore and said, 'How can I help?'

'Well, signor, can you tell me anything about Signor Nunienzo's personal life?'

'No, I don't think I can. I dealt with him remotely when I was booking the vacation – er, I mean holiday – and we only met him once when he handed over the keys.'

'Is that all you can tell me?'

'Yes, I kind of inferred that he has a large family or, rather was part of a large family, given the size of the house that we tried to knock up on Monday night.'

'*Scusi*, 'knock up'?'

'I mean that we were knocking at the front door for ages and there was no response. Mind you, it was the middle of the night so I'm sure everyone was asleep or else they thought we were there to do harm to them. We tried several times and Paolo had said to come any time but I guess that wasn't quite the case.'

'I see……were there any family members with Signor Nunienzo when he came over to give you the keys on Tuesday?'

'No, he was alone. Oh, I just thought – wonder who we give the keys back to when we leave?'

'I ask because Signor Nunienzo's older brother is missing. When we went over to let the family know what has happened his *mamma* was in tears already as the brother, Angelo, had been missing for two days.'

'Do you think that Angelo could be connected with the crime, Ispettore?'

'Not sure yet, but we will continue to investigate. *Grazie* for your help, Signor Wendell. I have one further request – may my team search this house for any clues that could help us?'

'Of course but let me tell my friend first. We can wait up on the roof deck if you like.'

'That would be fine…I will let the *ragazzi* in. Please be assured they will not destroy the house.'

'Thank you, *grazie*.'

Ten or so husky uniformed police filed in, all politely saying '*buon giorno*' to Mark, and proceeded to tear the place apart and then carefully put everything back together. Mark ran upstairs to the roof deck and told Andrew what was going on. Andrew put his head over the wall and saw that another crowd of locals had gathered with bulging eyes and tongues wagging at the obvious scandalous behavior of the neighbors.

Finally, after about thirty minutes the Ispettore came up to the roof deck and apologized profusely for any inconvenience. He took his leave gracefully, thanking the boys and the house was quiet, and the crowd melted away. Mark realized that he had not asked the Ispettore if anything had been found, but on descending to their bedrooms they found that their clothes had been searched and replaced immaculately, beds stripped and remade, bathroom cabinets dusted and then dusted off.

The guys decided to visit a local *osteria* for lunch called La Sosta Di Pio VII which was quite lovely. They sat outside under the gazebo which had ivy and flowers growing across it. It was a hot sunny day so they appreciated the shade. The food was delicious but the history of the place was more interesting – for one night Pope Pius VII on 2 June 1815 was forced to stop at the location by a "physical necessity". To this day the place is known locally as "the Pope's piss".

That night the guys dined at the second restaurant in the town square – Ristorante Triocco. Again, delicious food and atmosphere under the stars and a three-quarter moon. Crazy Bar was still closed. Mark wondered if it ever opened.

Chapter Five
Thursday

Mark was in the kitchen doing some of the boys' laundry when the doorbell rang just after 10:00 A.M. Surprised at a visitor at such an hour, he opened the front door to see Ispettore Garibaldi standing on the step looking immaculate as usual. There were no blue lights flashing in the street and no *ragazzi* standing around.

'*Buon giorno*, Ispettore. Please come in.'

'*Buon giorno*, signor.'

'How can I help you?'

'Well, for a start, may I have an espresso? For an American, you make espresso very well.'

Mark started the Keurig whilst secretly exulting inside at the compliment. Garibaldi was sitting at the table already and looked handsome, confident and sexy.

'Ummmm, so Ispettore, what can I do for you?'

'Please call me Massimo. It seems we are going to be spending more time together as this case progresses.'

Exultation.

'How is the case going – if you can tell me?'

'Well, we have a suspect in the guise of the brother, Angelo, but I'm not convinced that is the answer. If we could find him we'd be able to find out more, but Angelo Nunienzo has a record of larceny – although not of murder.'

'Mmmmmm – but what can I do to help?' said Mark.

'First may I have another espresso please?'

'Certainly,' said Mark, wondering where this conversation was going.

'We believe that Angelo might have been involved with the mob,' said Garibaldi.

'I thought that the Mafia had been almost eradicated in Italy?' said Mark.

'No, there are sadly local pockets and there might be one in Tavarnelle and there is definitely a cell in Poggibonsi.' Poggibonsi was a smallish industrial city to the south of Barberino.

'Okay – but where do I come in? I don't know anyone in the Mafia.'

'That's fine – we will get you an introduction to a half-way – I believe you call it a 'mole' in the U.S. – and get you recognized as an interested party. You may be able to find out information that can assist us. I would really appreciate it, and my colleague Andrea will provide protection for you. I would be too obvious to provide security for you. If you like, Andrea and I can take you to lunch and we can discuss.'

Exultation.

Mark ran upstairs to the roof deck and told Andrew he was going out with Massimo for lunch.

'Oooh – you have a crush on him, don't you?' said Andrew.

'No, don't be silly. Okay, maybe a little bit,' said Mark. 'But it's never going to go anywhere.'

Mark thought that Andrea referred to a man, but Andrea turned out to be a stunning woman, with long blonde hair either through nature or science, squished into skinny jeans, high heels and an almost see-through white blouse. She was quite the head-turner when she walked into the small restaurant in Tavarnelle where they had lunch with Massimo. After attending to the essentials of ordering appetizers and the main courses, as well as an impressive Super Tuscan wine, the team discussed the outline of the investigation. Andrea spoke flawless English and had a remarkable knowledge of police work. Mark asked Andrea what was her title and it turned out to be *Commandante* although Mark couldn't pronounce it correctly which led to peals of laughter at the table. She was from a different arm of Italian law enforcement which was fairly confusing.

The three agreed that Andrea would pick up Mark the next day and go to lunch with a couple of the Mafia boys that she was in contact with to see what she could find out. She thought that having Mark along would give her some credibility as a friend, not a police officer.

Massimo and Andrea dropped Mark off at the Airbnb after a leisurely and enjoyable three-hour lunch. Mark immediately went to bed for a post-prandial nap.

The boys decided to have dinner at the same restaurant they went to on Tuesday night. The Contessa greeted them and was dressed exquisitely in a black slub silk sleeveless dress of incredible and expensive simplicity. Since the evening was warm and not too humid, the boys decided to eat in the garden. The Contessa found a suitable table near the wire fence which prevented drunk *patroni* falling over the edge of the cliff, but afforded rich views of valleys, hills, olive groves, wine grapes growing and ruined castles.

After ordering food and wine, Mark said to Andrew, 'I have to go to the bathroom.' He walked up to the Contessa standing guard over her team on the stone-flagged patio. Mark thought he would try to speak more Italian.

'Contessa, *dov'è toilette?*'

The Contessa replied in flawless BBC English, 'No, dear, that's not how we say it. Go and pee and I'll teach you when you come back. It's that way,' pointing to the interior.

Mark was surprised that the Contessa would know to say 'pee' and realized, as he peed, that the Contessa was a more complex person than he gave her credit for, which was substantial. When returning to the patio the Contessa nodded and said:

'You say *dov'è sono I bagni*. That's the correct way.'

'*Grazie, signora.*'

The food was magnificent. The boys decided that this might be their favorite restaurant ever.

Chapter Six

Friday

Andrea arrived at the house with a luscious looking baby blue Lamborghini at 10:30 A.M. to pick up Mark to meet her 'associates' for lunch. Mark was impressed by the car but found it difficult to get his six-foot frame into a cramped although comfortable seat. Andrea looked every bit the supermodel in crisp black linen pants, a silver grey silk shirt and six-inch heels and slipped into the driving seat with elegance.

Before leaving, Mark had told Andrew what was happening and gave him Massimo's card so that if Mark didn't turn up again he could be contacted. Andrew was concerned that his friend could be hurt or worse, but Mark said that with Andrea around he felt safe. 'I'm sure she's packing heat somewhere although it's hard to see where she would put it.'

Andrea drove at an alarming speed to a restaurant in a little town called Marina di Bibbona near the coast of the Tyrrhenian Sea. They walked into an *osteria* called Anfora di Baratti overlooking the ocean and were shown to a table for five. They ordered aperitifs and were joined, punctually at noon, by two gentlemen in good quality suits and ties with expensive watches and wonderful shoes. They introduced themselves as Pietro Guardini and Stefano Farinelli. They did not seem to speak much English although appeared to be friendly so the conversation continued in rapid Italian until they were joined by the last guest, a rough-looking girl named Emilia. She seemed tense and edgy and uncomfortable. Andrea kicked Mark gently in the shin and looked harshly at him. He assumed that meant that he should pay attention to her. Mark immediately judged her to be using crystal meth, because after living in San Francisco for a few years he could recognize the signs.

At the meal the conversation was conducted primarily in Italian, and Mark was a little confused as to what was being discussed – although there were some passages concerning what Mark interpreted as business matters that he understood somewhat. Emilia started at the mention of 'Airbnb' and then resumed her taciturn demeanor. The meal ended around 3:00 P.M. with *digestivi* and espresso, much hugging and kissing and thanks.

Mark and Andrea climbed back in the Lamborghini but did not discuss anything that had happened until they arrived back in Barberino. The *commandante* left the car in the middle of the street, effectively blocking the narrow way. Mark supposed that she had some form of immunity, but left the front door open in case some other driver honked. After refusing another glass of wine, Andrea revealed that the girl Emilia was also the sister of the murdered Paolo, and although Andrea didn't state it directly it seemed that she suspected Emilia of being at the minimum involved in Paolo's death.

Chapter Seven
Saturday

The doorbell rang early at 8:30 A.M. and Andrew answered it.

'*Buon giorno*, Andrew. *Come va?* Is Marco around?' said Massimo.

Andrew said, 'No, he went out for a walk but he should be home soon.'

'If you don't mind I will wait for him.'

'Certainly – would you like a coffee?'

'*Si – ah grazie.*'

Massimo grimaced as he tasted the coffee but diplomatically said it was good. Mark arrived home about ten minutes later and, slightly sweaty and tired, was surprised to see Massimo.

Massimo said, 'Good morning, Marco. Where did you go for your walk?' squeezing Mark's shoulder quite hard as he stood up and towered above him. They both sat down at the kitchen table.

'Oh, just to the town square to listen to the church bells. It's funny, when I go for a walk in the mornings I always see an older lady walking around the churchyard. I always say '*buon giorno*' but up until now I just get a sneer. This morning I got a reluctant '*giorno*' and a sneer! It's a sign of luck, I think!' Mark immediately felt like an idiot and resolved to shut up.

'I guess you didn't want to see me again so soon.'

Mark felt a tugging at his heart strings. 'No, it's good to see you. And you are always welcome here.'

Massimo said, 'I am, *veramente*?'

'Yes, you're nice and…and…at least you shave every morning.'

'*Che cosa?*'

Mark was desperate to find a compliment or say at least something appropriate that didn't make him seem like a schoolgirl with a crush. 'Well, most men in their early thirties have scruff or beards and you don't. I like that.'

'*Grazie* and… I like you. *Mi piaci*. But there is something I need to discuss with you.'

'Okaaay???'

'Well, I spoke with Andrea after you went out yesterday and she's concerned that you guys might be in danger. Wait – no, don't speak. I'm not trying to scare you. But Paolo was your 'landlord', so to speak, and was found dead on your car and it seems Paolo's family is implicated. And so since Andrea is concerned for your safety and I am as well we want to keep some watch over you.'

Mark was confused and said, 'How do you mean "keeping watch"? Like being guarded or have a GPS device attached or something?'

Massimo laughed. 'No *caro*, just let me hang around every so often and Andrea and her team will discreetly follow you when you guys go out.'

'Oh, okay…but I'm a little freaked out by this.'

'Don't be…..we won't let anything happen to you and Andrew.'

'Ummm. Thanks.'

'Okay, I have to go. But I will see you later *questa sera*.'

Massimo stood to leave and gave Mark a hug. Mark thought he smelled wonderful, like Aqua di Parma and soap.

Andrew came downstairs after Massimo had left and made obnoxious kissing sounds to tease Mark. 'Shut up,' said Mark. 'Come on, let's go and do something today.'

The boys ended up driving to San Gimignano and upon entering the *centro storico*, Mark was enchanted by the towers, the squat limestone cathedral and the ambience of the people, markets and the cobblestoned streets. They saw a cute-looking restaurant earlier in the day in the Via San Matteo that they thought might be good for lunch. Just after noon, when they felt hunger pangs attacking, they descended a couple of steps and entered the restaurant. The waiter almost shouted *'chiuso!'* and the boys retreated, wondering why they should be shut at this time. They wandered a little further down the street, not having another option in mind, and found another restaurant where the menu posted outside the building seemed simple and very good.

Andrew and Mark walked in and Mark said to the owner, '*Aprire, Signor?*' hoping that was polite. The owner replied in perfect English, 'Yes gentlemen, just two? Do you want to sit on the *loggia?*' The boys agreed and were shown enthusiastically to a table under an umbrella with a ravishing view of the red bricks and magical towers of San Gimignano. It was a fantastic setting and lunch turned out to be sensational. Mark enjoyed a pasta dish of *pici* with walnuts and blue cheese. It was simple and delicious.

Massimo dropped into the house later that evening and they regaled him over wine, beer and mineral water on the roof deck with their tales of the beauty and history of San Gimignano. Massimo must have heard this from foreigners before but was graceful and listened attentively.

At the end of the evening he stood up and took his leave with an extra strong hug and promised to check in on the guys tomorrow afternoon. Andrew teased Mark a little more about Massimo and Mark took it good-naturedly, but again, wondered if anything would come of it.

Chapter Eight
Sunday

There were no early morning visitors on Sunday morning although the bells from the church in the village went crazy at 7:00 A.M. and continued all morning. Mark was enchanted and walked up to the church in the square, peeked inside and saw a service being conducted. With the candles, the stained glass and the choir singing it was a magical scene. On the way around the village Mark didn't see the old lady that had sneered at him previously... she was presumably at worship. Mark hoped that she had a black knitted shawl across her head.

When he got home, Andrew said that they should just go for a drive and see where fate took them. Mark was fine with that, showered, shaved and changed into better clothes in case they ended up somewhere fancy for lunch.

The boys started off driving towards the mountains that they had passed over a week before. They drove to Poggibonsi, Castellino in Chianti, Radda in Chianti – which looked very suitable for lunch but the one restaurant was not yet open – and finally, a little lost but delighted, found an *Osteria* sign that pointed down a dirt track. Mark told Andrew, who was driving, to take it as he was feeling adventurous and hungry. They came to a beautiful old farm house but the road continued and finally ended up at a car park.

Mark said, 'This must be the place.'

Andrew, rolling his eyes, was clearly underwhelmed and said, 'What makes you say that?' All they could see was an old derelict-looking red wooden barn but with a magical view in the distance.

'Because there's a bunch of Range Rovers and a Bentley or two with British plates. They know a good restaurant when they see one.'

The boys walked up to the barn/restaurant which was called Vignale and it turned out to be a modernized interior tucked into medieval rafters and limestone walls and was totally charming. It was packed but the boys got a table for two and sat down to enjoy. Mark had *cinghiale* for the first time and Andrew had ravioli filled with ricotta and truffle butter.

Stuffed with excellent food and some wine, the boys walked back to the car and drove back to Barberino, with a few missed turns in the small twisting roads in the mountains. It was a wonderful experience, with every turn revealing new vistas.

Arriving home, they found a note from Andrea tucked under the front door asking Mark to meet her at Crazy Bar that afternoon at 5:00 P.M. He was somewhat surprised but thought it was a fairly normal request. He wondered how she would get the Lamborghini into the small main street but if anyone could do it, Andrea could.

At 5:00 P.M. Mark entered the previously darkened Crazy Bar which, surprisingly, was open. It was a bit of a dive, but had a fantastic view over the Chianti valleys and hills which was entrancing. He ordered a glass of wine served in a small tumbler and the bartender disappeared. The music on the electronic jukebox was loud and pulsating, some songs in Italian and others in English. There were no other patrons in the bar at that time and Mark, not for the first time, did not doubt that the name Crazy Bar was appropriate.

Mark had no notice of the blow from behind that descended on him and knocked him out. The world went black.

Chapter Nine
Monday

Mark woke up in a strange dark bedroom which was dirty and clearly distressed, with a raging headache and a desperate thirst. He looked around and couldn't see a bathroom or a tap and feeling nauseous, tried to go back to sleep. He fell back asleep with very bizarre dreams.

A few hours later the door opened and a young girl with dirty fingers and lank dark hair entered with a tray which had a bottle of water and a bowl of minestrone. She was silent and Mark said, 'Where am I?' which clearly the girl did not understand. She went out of the door and Mark could hear the lock being turned.

Mark ate and drank hungrily. The minestrone was average but Mark didn't expect a 5-star experience.

'What the hell happened?' thought Mark. He walked over to the window which was dirty but he wiped some of the muck off with the threadbare blanket on the bed. It appeared that he was on a farm and on the second floor. There were sheep and cows wandering around or lying on the grass in the sun or under trees. He discovered a filthy toilet in a corner which made him feel like a prisoner in a bad jail movie but was desperately needed.

Towards the middle of the afternoon he was feeling hungry again and began to wonder what had happened to his phone which he could not find. He guessed it dropped on to the floor of Crazy Bar when he was attacked. Just then, he heard some pops and angry voices, apparently coming from downstairs. He tried the door but it was still locked firmly. The pops continued and Mark thought they might have been gunshots and he ran across to the window to see if he could see what was going on. The cows and sheep gave him no indication.

The gunshots subsided and Mark could hear boots on a stairway and a muddle of voices. The lock on the door was being turned and Mark felt alarm that it might be the people who had kidnapped him. The door opened and Mark was prepared to defend himself, but didn't quite know how. It turned out to be Andrea, looking like a million dollars in boots, jeans and a crisp white shirt with a black leather jacket on top. She was accompanied by three hulking policemen covering Mark and each other with Berettas.

'Andrea, what's going on? How did I get here?'

'Marco, you were kidnapped and were being held for ransom.'

Mark, confused, asked, 'Ransom, what the hell? I don't understand…'

Andrea gave orders to the *ragazzi* and they departed downstairs. 'Mark, you appeared at lunch the other day, which was my fault, but it brought the Mafia out and we found out that Emilia planned this attack so she could get more money for her …..umm…..*abitudine*. 'Habit', I think in English?'

'But who would have paid the ransom? And what was I worth?' Mark felt shallow for asking but was interested to know.

'The U.S. Embassy in Roma and about a million.' Andrea tossed her long blonde hair and walked out the door. 'Come on, we're taking you to the hospital. *Andiamo*.'

Mark followed and looked around in wonder at the very dirty and untended farm house which looked like it hadn't been maintained in three centuries. He walked downstairs a little wobbly and Andrea helped him to get in the car. A black and white Peugeot this time, not the Lamborghini. They drove to a local tiny hospital where the *dottore* checked him for concussion which proved to be correct, wrapped a pretty ineffectual bandage around his head, and told Andrea that Mark was free to go. They had a rapid conversation in Italian which Mark couldn't understand.

Andrea and her second-in-command sat in the front seat of the Peugeot and Mark was stuffed into the back seat between two muscly uniformed officers, in pale blue polos and blue camo pants, which wasn't entirely unpleasant. Mark had no idea where he was but after about twenty minutes they arrived back in Barberino. Mark felt he might have some new bruises on his ribs after the guys pulled him out of the car and they put their hands under his arm pits and basically lifted him into the house. Andrew was there looking worried and in the background was Massimo.

'Where the heck have you been?' asked Andrew.

'I honestly do not know…..Andrea?'

Massimo came over and hugged Mark hard and led him to the sofa. 'Sit, sit. There's time enough for talk.' Mark was very aware that he must smell bad and wished he could have gone upstairs and had a shower and brushed his teeth while he sat next to the man he was falling in love with. 'Yes,' he told himself, 'I love him. How silly is that? He lives in Italy and I live in America.' But he was still a bit wobbly and didn't know if he could get up the stairs to the bathroom without being pathetic and crawling up the stairs. With Massimo, Andrea, the three hulking cheerful *polizie* and Andrew busily making drinks or opening wine and Nastro Azzuros he didn't think he could pull it off. There were lots of discussions going on in a mixture of Italian and

English and they were getting louder and more excited. Mark's head buzzed a little.

Andrew brought him a glass of *pinot grigio* and Massimo a beer. Massimo laid his arm around Mark's shoulders.

More exultation. It just felt right, thought Mark.

'I suspect you have some questions,' said Massimo.

'Ummmmm….yes, a lot.' Try to be logical, Mark, he said to himself.

'I'll say…how the heck do you always get yourself into trouble?' said Andrew.

Andrea said, '*Cosi*, the unlovely Emilia killed Paolo because he owned this house himself and she wanted to fund her habit. So she kidnapped you with the assistance of her Mafia *amici* and was going to hold you for ransom for a million as she knew you were staying at Paolo's Airbnb. It was insurance in case the murder of her brother didn't work out.'

'But the U.S. government would never pay a ransom of a million dollars!' said Mark.

'A million Euro, dear. About 1.2 million dollars.'

'Wow, you're worth that much?' said Andrew. 'That's ridiculous.'

'Thanks very much,' said Mark. 'But why me?'

'Because you're American and those *Mafiosi* think that all Americans are rich and vulnerable to extortion,' said Andrea. Massimo agreed. 'But what made you go to Crazy Bar, Marco?'

'Because I saw the note from Andrea under the door when I got home! It told me to go there at 5 o'clock.'

'That wasn't from me, darling. That was Emilia faking a note from me. She knew me from lunch the other day and recognized that I was police. Why didn't you call my *cellulare*?'

'Oh.' Mark felt incredibly stupid.

'So we came over here and Andrew told us that you had gone to Crazy Bar. We went there and it was closed but we broke in. When you weren't there we tracked you down to a place that we knew Emilia sometimes went to. We have arrested Emilia and she's under charges of kidnapping and *furto*. The police will prosecute for the kidnapping and the *Guardia Finanza* will prosecute for the *furto*. How do you say in English?'

'Larceny,' said Massimo.

'And then there is a charge of her brother's murder but that will have to go through a *giudice per l'udienza preliminare*.'

After a little while Mark asked Massimo if he would help him up to the bedroom, which went better than expected. Massimo discreetly left as Mark went into the bathroom to have a shower and brush his teeth and fell on top of the bed in a change of underwear. He slept soundly for a couple of hours, and woke up and heard no sounds downstairs, although a couple of voices were coming faintly from the roof deck. Mark slipped on shorts and a T-shirt and walked downstairs and saw the detritus of beer and wine bottles and coffee cups. He felt a little like he was hungover and couldn't face cleaning that up, but he grabbed a clean wine glass and headed up to the roof deck where he thought Andrew and Massimo might have been hanging out.

Andrew and Massimo were on the roof deck chatting ten to the dozen and Mark slipped into Massimo's arm as he poured Mark a glass of wine. 'What are you talking about?' asked Mark. 'Italian football, I mean 'soccer',' said Andrew. 'I just don't understand why the players are so dramatic.'

'That's just part of the Italian *psiche*,' said Massimo. Mark interpreted that as 'psyche'. 'It's just the way we are. Dramatic but we mean it.'

'What time is it?' asked Mark practically, as his stomach rumbled.

'It's 7:00 P.M.' said Massimo. 'Why, are you hungry, Marco?'

'Massimo, how do you know what I'm thinking all the time?' asked Mark.

'Well, because I like you a lot and I like food – and eating in Italy is a central part of our lives.'

'Yes, I am starving. Andrew, let's go to the Contessa's! We haven't eaten our way through the entire menu just yet. Massimo, there's a great restaurant just down the street. We can walk there.'

Andrew was on board and Massimo agreed. 'Do you mean Il Paese dei Campanelli?'

'Yes, but how did you know? I thought you were from Florence?'

'That place is famous. It's won numerous awards. Sounds good.'

Mark and Andrew changed into more suitable clothes, and the three made their way to the restaurant and were greeted by the Contessa as usual with style and grace, wearing an exquisitely cut navy blue blazer and white skirt, looking exactly like a marketing campaign for a couture Ralph Lauren maritime collection. The Contessa wore a single piece of jewellery tonight, a substantial diamond cuff which glinted and glistened under the restaurant lights.

She sat the three men down at a table inside as it looked as though it might rain, and handed them menus. Massimo and the Contessa conducted a rapid conversation in Italian with many hand gestures which Mark and Andrew failed to follow but ended with smiles all around. 'What was that all about, Massimo?' said Mark.

'We were just discussing the *speciali* for this evening. They have a *tonno* and a special Florentine steak.'

Mark had seen the size of Florentine steaks and decided he couldn't face that much red meat so ordered the *tonno*, Andrew chose the white pizza again, and Massimo had a smaller steak cooked to a surprising shade of red. 'I like rare!' he explained with a shrug. Massimo had red wine, Mark had *pinot grigio* and Andrew drank Pellegrino *aqua minerale*.

The evening passed very pleasantly but a thought overtook Mark when he realized that they only had one more day in Barberino before he and Andrew were due to return to Florence and fly back to Barcelona and then the States. Had this whole thing with Massimo just been a holiday romance? He hoped not but couldn't see any future here, given the geographic difference.

After dinner, the three walked back to the house and then decided to have a drink at The Bar. They passed through the Siena Gate, saw Crazy Bar on the right which caused Mark to shiver a little, then through the Florence Gate and took up a table on the patio of The Bar, facing the old women and the graveyard. It was a beautiful moon-lit evening with many stars in the skies.

Mark walked inside and asked the *patrona* for a liter of wine and a glass of sparkling mineral water for Andrew. He turned around, saw the old men playing checkers outside, asked for another liter of wine and several glasses. He took that out to the old gentlemen who were surprised and delighted before coming back into the bar to get their own drinks. '*Signora, dove vieno questo vino?*' hoping that sounded al-most correct. The woman gestured vaguely down the hillside outside the windows and said '*laggiù*' which Mark took to mean that it couldn't have been more local. '*Grazie, signora.*' Together the wine and mineral water had cost less than € 10.

When Mark walked outside to their table the old women were walking across the road from the graveyard scowling at him for in-fluencing their men and getting them drunk. There were several argu-ments starting and some of the more hen-pecked husbands disgustedly followed their spouses home. Others were steadfast and told their women to leave them alone, leading to more scowling at Mark.

'What did you do, Marco?' asked Massimo, aware of the tension.

'Nothing,' said Mark, feeling that nothing could spoil this even-ing. Finally, peace was restored and the old ladies who remained were back on their perches in the cemetery.

'So Massimo, I still have some questions about what happened and I'm sorry that I'm a little foggy.'

'*Si*, ask away,' said Massimo.

'Was it Emilia who killed her brother?'

'Yes, with the assistance of the Mafia boys. You're lucky that you weren't more caught up in it than you were.'

'But what happened to the brother, Angelo?'

'Oh, he turned up….he'd gone to his girlfriend's in Corsica for a few days but didn't tell his *mamma*.'

'Oh. Well. I know I don't exactly have a great family but we stop short of killing each other.'

'Yes, that is what addiction will do to you. Emilia was hoping to get the proceeds from the house or your ransom. Or both.'

On that sad note, the guys sat back in relative silence and enjoyed the beauty of the Tuscan evening.

'So what happened to my cell phone that I lost at Crazy Bar?' asked Mark, after an interval. 'Not that I have missed it at all, but was just wondering.'

'Oh, one of the policemen returned it yesterday. It's at home,' said Andrew.

'I hate to say this but we probably need to get on the computer tonight and check in for our flight tomorrow,' said Mark to Andrew. Massimo was staring off into the distance and looked stern. Mark felt that he had dropped a time bomb.

'Massimo….' said Mark.

'Yes?'

'I don't want to go. I want to see you more….' Mark said, feeling lame.

'I want the same, Marco….but we both know that's not going to work.'

The three walked home in complete silence, all of them grateful that it was only a five-minute walk.

Andrew walked upstairs to his bedroom, discreetly leaving Mark and Massimo alone.

'I wish this was easier,' said Mark.

'I know........*mi mancherai davvero e vorrei che potessimo stare insieme*. Sorry, I didn't know how to say that in English.'

'You did a pretty good job in Italian though. You've done a pretty good job all around.' Lame, Mark, lame!

'You made it easier. *Sei tutto per me*.'

Okay, Mark thought. I'm either going to become a sobbing mess or I can treat this with dignity and respect. Can I do both? He thought facetiously. No, no, focus on Massimo please. Mark's right side and left side of the brain argued with themselves and his heart and stomach seemed to join in as willing participants. He felt nauseous.

Massimo left and promised to see Mark in the morning. 'But Massimo, you don't want to come down here from Florence just to go back to the airport,' said Mark.

'Yes, I do, and I know a few back roads to the airport. You see, that's my home. See you in the morning.' He bent down and gave Mark a kiss on the forehead which was so much better than on the lips, although Mark was just trying to forestall him leaving.

'Massimo, do you want to stay the night?'

'No, *caro*, I don't think that would be a good idea. I would love to, but it's useless to hurt ourselves further.'

'I understand. *Buona sera*, Massimo.'

'*Buona notte*, Marco.'

Chapter Ten
Tuesday

The next morning started early with the boys packing and lugging suitcases downstairs, cleaning up the house and emptying the rubbish and recyclables to the appropriate receptacles outside. They left the key under the mat in the approved fashion, as Paolo wasn't around anymore.

When the guys walked their suitcases and backpacks down to where the Mercedes was parked, they were surprised to find that there were a couple of police Peugeots, an Alfa Romeo and a baby blue Lamborghini all milling around. The cops were standing around smoking and chatting.

Massimo jumped out of the Alfa and hugged Mark. '*Buon giorno,* Marco and Andrew.'

'Ummm, what's going on, Massimo?' said Mark.

'We're giving you an escort to the airport. Thought it might be fun.'

'Okaaayyy…..but we have to return the car to the rental office.'

'Si, si. That's *perfetto.*'

Andrew and Mark loaded the luggage and climbed into the Mercedes in some confusion and started the car. Andrea drove relatively slowly, for her, and her Lamborghini led the way, followed by Massimo's

Alfa, the Mercedes and the black-and-whites following along behind. They hit the Si-Fi highway and the Peugeots turned on the blue lights and the Lamborghini sped up. Andrew had some difficulty following at a fast but respectable and safe distance and they arrived at Peretola airport in about twenty minutes. The day was taking on a dreamlike atmosphere, unreal and fantastic.

Mark and Andrew got to the rental office and handed the keys back to the agent behind the counter whose eyes were bulging with excitement or fear seeing the cop cars and the Lamborghini outside. The officers bundled the luggage into the Peugeots and Mark climbed in beside Massimo in the Alfa and Andrew got in the Lamborghini next to Andrea.

'Massimo, I'm a little overwhelmed at the moment…' said Mark.

'I know, *caro*, I know. That's Italy for you!'

'So I'm starting to understand.'

'Does that mean you will come back and see more of Italy? And perhaps me?'

'Definitely yes.' Exultation again. Apparently today was a full schedule of emotions for Mark.

They arrived at the terminal, again in a very short time, and Andrea, Massimo and the officers left their cars scattered all over the departure level to the raised eyebrows of passengers and airport staff. They walked inside, the *carabinieri* carried their suitcases inside and left them at the first class counter, to the raised eyebrows and pursed lips of the check-in agent. Andrew and Mark checked their suitcases and they went to Security. Andrea, Massimo and the officers showed their official badges and walked through with obvious weapons on display. Mark had never seen such a thing before and idly wondered if this was at all legal.

Mark and Andrew got a full-body search by scared yet impressed security agents and were told '*grazie*, Signore'. They went to the gate and time passed extremely rapidly. Mark and Andrew stood up when the flight boarding was announced, were hugged by everyone with tears and rapid Italian compliments. When they joined the passenger line everyone except Massimo discreetly remained seated chatting amongst themselves.

'*Arrivederci, caro,*' said Massimo. He kissed Mark on the forehead again. Mark thought he was going to implode.

'Bye, Massimo….I love you.'

'I love you more, Marco. *Ti amo.*'

'Always with me, always with you.'

'*Che cosa?*' said Massimo.

'Google it.'

Mark and Andrew boarded the plane and after a delay with other passengers boarding, some with stares at the boys, it took off into a beautiful sunny day headed to Barcelona.

Andrew finally ended the silence after they had got their first drink and said, 'Well, you're a bit of a slut aren't you?' He smiled, enjoying the teasing.

'What? I don't think so.'

'Yeah right. But I had a good time – I loved the food, the history and especially that ride in the Lamborghini.'

'We'll be back,' said Mark.

The plane kept flying smoothly towards Barcelona through the afternoon sunlight with the glistening Mediterranean below.

The End